Forget it Felix

Paul Abdool

Illustrated by Eugene Kim

Forget it Felix
Copyright © 2020 by Paul Abdool

All rights reserved. No part of this publication may be reproduced, distributed, or transmitted in any form or by any means, including photocopying, recording, or other electronic or mechanical methods, without the prior written permission of the author, except in the case of brief quotations embodied in critical reviews and certain other non-commercial uses permitted by copyright law.

Tellwell Talent
www.tellwell.ca

ISBN
978-0-2288-4527-0 (Hardcover)
978-0-2288-4528-7 (Paperback)
978-0-2288-4790-8 (eBook)

Dedicated to the inspiration for the book, my son Kai, who is like many little boys who forget.

A big thanks for the love and support of my parents; my daughter; and my wife, my partner in child-rearing, who has read many books to the kids and knows what other little ones would like to hear.

Felix was a six-year-old boy who was very curious and helpful.
His mind was on many things.

Felix thought about rockets, playing with his friends, after-school activities, and toys with bouncy springs.

With so many things on his mind, Felix was easily distracted.

He was so distracted that he often forgot what he was just in the middle of doing.

Felix forgot stuff; it was starting to get tough.

Felix forgot his water bottle on the kitchen counter when he went to practice.

After skating around for a while, his mouth felt like a dry desert cactus.

Felix forgot his school bag in the family car.

Without it, his homework would not get very far.

Felix forgot his gloves at the arena in the change room.

When his mom found out, she yelled like a sonic boom.

Felix didn't really like to get up for school in the morning.

He sat in his comfortable bed, with thoughts of his day running around in his head.

The later he got up, the more he forgot, since he was always running around an awful lot.

Felix never missed his school bus, but he often forgot to do all of the things that his parents asked him to.

Felix forgot his homework in his room.

He knew that school would be doom and gloom.

Felix forgot his lunchbox at school.

He knew it was right by the turtle's pool.

Felix forgot his soccer ball on the school bus.

He knew his dad would make a serious fuss.

Felix forgot to put things back where they belonged.

He had trouble finishing tasks. Where did he go wrong?

Maybe his mind was too busy with exciting things all day long.

Or was he just being a kid, having fun and singing a new song?

Felix forgot the milk and bread on the counter.

He wanted to puddle-jump in the rain shower.

Felix forgot to turn off the TV.

He was distracted when he saw a really, really big bumblebee.

Felix forgot his empty plate on the table.

He forgot his cowboy hat in the stable.

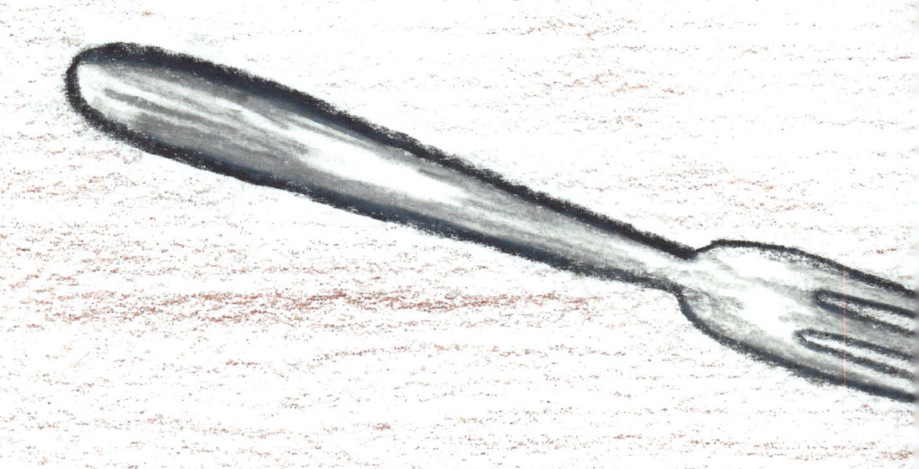

Felix forgot to do the things that were important for his health and well-being.

His teeth and dirty hands didn't always get a good cleaning.

Felix forgot about his boring duties and tiring chores.

He would much rather watch sports and check out the scores.

Felix forgot to put away his clean laundry.

He was too busy playing a video game. His mom was in a quandary.

Upset about forgetting things, Felix wanted to improve.

Everyone would be happy if he could just get in a groove.

Felix knew he needed some advice.

So he asked some people who would be supportive and nice.

Felix wanted to remember his water bottle. So he asked his mom, "What would you do to remember your water?"

She said, "I would make a _checklist_ of everything that I needed to take, so I won't forget and have to give my head a shake."

STOP AND LOOK AROUND

Felix wanted to remember his bag when he left the car. So he asked his dad, "What would you do to remember your bag?"

He said, "When I get out of the car, I would _stop and look around_ to see if anything was left behind waiting to be found."

Felix didn't like forgetting things he should do before school.

He also didn't like forgetting important things he needed for class on a stool.

He really wanted to improve but he wasn't sure how to get better.

There were no rules or a monthly newsletter.

Felix decided to ask some people who were smart.

They seemed to always remember; they knew it all by heart.

Felix often forgot his homework at home; it sometimes drove him berserk.

So he asked his dad, "How do you remember to take things with you to work?"

His dad said, "I *prepare* all my things the night before.

Then, I leave them by the front door.

I find it easier to do this preparation before bed.

Rushing around in the morning makes me forget all the things in my head."

PREPARE

Felix wondered about how he could remember things when he could not prepare.

Things like his soccer ball on the school bus; he really did care.

So he asked his sister, "How do you remember your things when you get off the bus, without any preparation or making a fuss?"

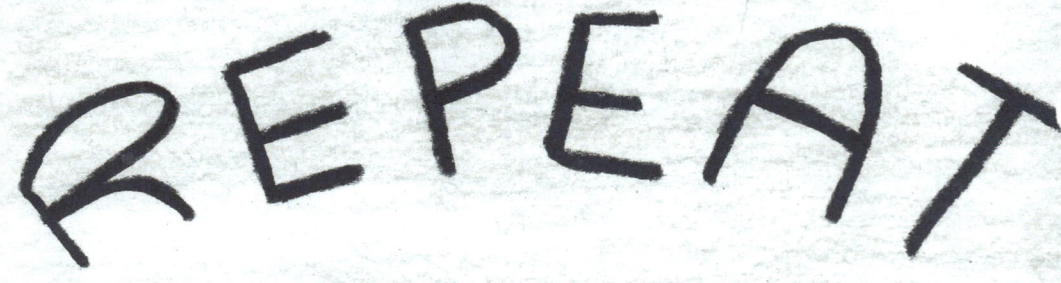

His sister said, "I try to put my things in the same place every time.

I _repeat_ the same action, like an actor practices for a show. The action repeats in my head like an echo in the valley below."

She added, "I put my basketball on my lap or by my feet.

When I move, I remember it, as soon as I get out of my seat."

Felix didn't like when his mom had to keep reminding him; in fact, he knew it was wrong.

He wanted to remember to put things back where they belong.

Felix didn't like making his mom upset.

He really, really wanted to remember not to forget.

Felix wanted to remember to put away the cheese.

So he asked his dad, "How do you remember to clean up with such ease?"

His dad said, "Some things that I do over and over have formed a good _habit_.

It takes a few weeks; change is not as quick as a rabbit.

So every time I cut some cheese and put it on a plate, the block of cheese goes right back in the fridge nice and straight."

Felix wanted to remember to put his empty plate and glass in the dishwasher. So he asked his mom, "How do you remember to put your dishes in the dishwasher?"

His mom said, "For me, it's easy to _take responsibility_. If I use a plate, a spoon, and a cup, I take them all to the dishwasher when I get up."

Felix felt like there were so many things to remember and he was feeling a lot of stress.

However, he liked when he did remember to do things without having to guess.

Felix decided to ask his family for some ideas to help him remember his daily chores and things that he should do before he went to bed on the second floor.

Felix wanted to remember to brush his teeth before he went to bed. So he asked his sister, "How do you remember to brush your teeth every night?"

His sister said, "I remember because I have a _routine_ every night before I go to bed and turn out the light."

Felix said, "That sounds a lot like a habit that dad was talking about."

ROUTINE

A habit is something we do often in the same way.

A routine is doing things step by step each day.

"So before I go to bed:

Step 1 - I put away my homework
Step 2 - I put on my pjs and then
Step 3 - I brush my teeth…that's my routine.

You just have to _practice_ and soon you will remember and be clean."

Felix said, "I get it! I see what you mean."

Felix is not the only one on the planet to forget things.

Every day, people forget—even queens and kings.

The good news is you can learn how to remember by always doing your part.

Create habits and routines, and practice them until you know them by heart.

Ways to remember list:

- Checklists
- Stop and look around
- Prepare
- Repetition
- Habits
- Take responsibility
- Routine
- Practice

Printed in the USA
CPSIA information can be obtained
at www.ICGtesting.com
LVHW070039250823
756176LV00019B/1142